Nightmares

For Greg

Contents

Junkie

The conversation has been flowing, like the wine, and now that
Claire has touched his hand over dessert, he thinks the whole
thing galvanised - that is, as a *good date*. One that will surely lead
to another, at least. And Matthew is pleased, takes a sip of his
sauvignon, not before performing with it: the customary twirl of
liquid around the glass, the obligatory huff of its vapours; a non-
habit, of course, to lose in the earliest realms of coupling. But not
yet - now, a tool for creating a subconscious sense (or perhaps
reassurance) of sophistication. A sense that will transcend memory
of the event: a mnemonic 'in spite of-' for later dirtiness. First
impressions and all that.

And Claire is smiling, holding her glass, and giggling, tries to drink
from it a third time, prevented by Matthew: two remarks, twice
laughter, commentary on his doing this. Third laughter - exhausted
now. The game dictates she gets the fourth. And she sips her iced
sauvignon as an exposed part of her leg brushes his jean, and they
look into one another's eyes. But she knows that this is a first date -
a good date - but nonetheless too early for seriousness; best to keep
things light-hearted.

So Claire asks Matthew: "what was the one thing that turned you off about my profile?" because they have already discussed the converse and because she will say his small sausage hands. Particularly, his small sausage hands in the one with the Japanese Spider Crab where they looked even more so holding that enormous exoskeleton. Claire will say his little sausage hands because sausagey hands are a benign reference and no doubt attributes of Matthew she will later come to love. Imperfections are the greatest perfections and all that.

And Matthew pauses for a second and giggles. His giggling acts as a sort of probe into her psyche that her giggling back absolves. And Matthew thinks as he holds his glass of new world, and thinks in an overemphasised manner that causes Claire to laugh, also, knowing too quick an answer will breed self-consciousness. So he deliberates out of politeness, and after some time: "well, if I had to say something... I guess referring to yourself as a travel junkie. I mean, unless you're Indiana Jones or something... everyone enjoys holidays; you're not a junkie for going to Bali three years in a row!". And he giggles again, this time unmet.

And Claire turns pale, crumples into her desk job hunch, looks down at the Tarte Tatin, stifles a cry.

And Matthew, with all the tepidness of his demographic: "Did I say something wrong?"

"No, no," Claire insists. Nothing *wrong*. It's the truth, of course, that hurts.

"Claire" says Matthew, putting out his hand.

Which she doesn't take, and breathes to calm. Eventually says, "Matthew. There's something I should tell you. Before we do all this".

And she says it with sort of despairing laughter. *Here we go again, Claire*. And by this, she means their coupling, although gestures with her pastry fork, a circle around the uneaten Tarte Tatin. A metaphor, maybe.

"Ple-ase," he chokes.

And she decides she will take him up on that hand. And says: "Matthew. I'm a travel-a-holic", with a face so serious he cannot entertain the possibility that this is some joke - a clunky attempt at early familiarity. And his face must show it because she reiterates "a fucking travel junkie," and Matthew's heart beats faster now.

"..."

"When it's bad, I'll do anything to go travelling. Suck your cock for a lift to Peterborough, if only I hadn't been".

"Claire I don't-, what?" says Matthew.

"Always getting from A to B, is Claire," she snaps. "Held onto a lorry exhaust the other week because I heard it was going to Mapledurham. *Fucking Mapledurham*".

"I-"

"Spent my grandmother's inheritance on Ryanair and neck pillows-"

"But-"

"Got a tenner for the Megabus?"

Knights of the realm

Ian Langtree is a 51-year-old insurance broker from Twyford, near Reading. He has three young children and a cat. The cat lives with him. The three young children live in Bath with their mother, Emily, and her new partner, and their cat. Ian Langtree rarely sees the three young children because neither Emily nor Dan drive. Dan (Emily's new partner) considers himself a hippy in this respect.

Currently, Ian Langtree is cycling as fast as he can towards an oncoming van. In his right hand, he grips an 8ft galvanised steel scaffold pole that he rests on the handlebar of his bicycle as an improvised lance. In the oncoming van, leant out of the driver's window, holding a galvanised steel scaffold pole of similar proportions (also lance-like), is Peter Downes, a 43-year-old self-employed scaffolder from Reading. It is Peter Downes' van. These are Peter Downes' tools. On a nearby lawn, slumped in a state of minor concussion, oscillating between fiction and fact, lies Peter Downes' 18-year-old son, Toby. Toby Downes, or *the fat son*, is currently being tended to by Mal White's daughter-in-law for a nasty head injury. Toby Downes works with his father during the summer holidays. It is the summer holidays now. It is the 28th of July of that year.

Twenty metres is all that remains between the two men. Ian Langtree has achieved a top speed of 13mph. The bicycle will decelerate before the impending inevitable. The van has reached a speed of 25mph. The van is accelerating. With such closing velocity, there is already ample capacity for the incoming scaffold poles to incur massive and irrevocable damage to both vehicle and/or human(s). Onlookers look on aghast. They wonder what could compel these two adult men to pull such a stunt, steeped in all its potential dangers. Some marvel at their willingness to sacrifice tissue for the sake of ideology. But no one really knows what is going on. Everyone is scared.

*

Our story starts with Ian Langtree's divorce and separation from his three young children and spouse, and the subsequent period of his life where he came to realise he no longer had any friends or hobbies, and how the last 15 years had distracted him from this fact. In the six months following the divorce, after moving into a maisonette in Twyford, Ian Langtree discovered free time again. Free time was not as good as he had remembered it. It was sometimes quite lonely, for instance. And sometimes it was hard to fill, and he certainly never remembered this from before, and on the contrary, he remembered it always being filled even before he wished to fill it.

He had taken up golfing with colleagues. But he did not like golf, nor was he capable at it, and the three weekends or so he had played it - mostly the time spent on the green, but also, the mid-week 'water cooler' banter - reminded him of his grammar school, where he had not liked rugby either, and how he had spent those seven years feeling like he could never really access the inner circle, the real social core of the school, because of this, despite his perceived prowesses elsewhere. Golf reminded him of rugby at grammar school because it reminded him that he was at heart an outsider and not someone who could truly fit in and that even when it appeared he was fitting in, it would never amount to more than this appearance.

Fortunately, Ian Langtree's divorce occurred in the era of fibre optic broadband and the PC. In the six months following his divorce, during which time Ian Langtree discovered he no longer had any real friends or hobbies, Ian Langtree also discovered the seemingly endless possibilities at his fingertips with a mouse and keyboard. For instance, he discovered movie pirating and that it was easy, and that it wasn't such a bad thing to do after all (every film it seemed was available online with the right google search and a sturdy anti-virus package). He learnt to brew his own beer and cook steak the proper way. He discovered free internet pornography. He trawled through message boards dedicated to his favourites series' and learnt to diagnose maladies without going to the doctor. He could even see how Emily was getting on in Bath with Dan and the three young children, by reading their frequent and readily available updates on Facebook. Indeed, the PC afforded Ian Langtree a rich range of possibilities in the period of time after his divorce. It became the friend and hobby to replace what he'd lost, and went some way in filling the void he experienced in those first few months.

*

On the first christmas after his divorce, Ian Langtree received a GoPro camera from his brother and his brother's wife. It was £135 more expensive than the gift he bought them; a crate of eight 'interesting beers'.

*

Studies show that internet users can be approximately divided into two categories describing macro-level patterns of online behaviour. One category describes the behaviour of an estimated 95% of the internet user base, the other, the remaining 5%. Experts label the two categories 'Consumers' and 'Producers' respectively.

Like most people, Ian Langtree started out using the internet as a consumer. A consumer consumes: both information and entertainment. A consumer watches videos on Youtube. They read online travel blogs and download music. A consumer googles the nearest Nando's, or orders pizza. A consumer such as Ian Langtree does not upload acoustic covers. A consumer such as Ian Langtree does not have a fashion blog or a Tumblr or 'an app'. He is not what the experts describe as a pro-active social media engager (a consumer will interact with social media, but: "relatively infrequently, and with a smaller demographic of persons whom they will mostly know from the real world."). The consumer sits and scrolls and stares, leaving little trace of their activities. Producers, on the other hand, that 5% minority of internet users, create the content the rest of the 95% enjoy.

*

7

On the first boxing day after his divorce, Ian Langtree receives a generously dishonest comment from a member of his sister-in-law's family: "you should really think about making your own Youtube videos; you could be good at that". Ian Langtree blushes and sips a buck's fizz and thinks.

In the aftermath of his divorce, Ian Langtree bought an expensive bicycle and took to cycling to and from work in an attempt to get fitter, as well as to remove some of the soft fat amassing exclusively around his abdomen that contrasted his storkish legs, and eclipsed his limp penis hanging beneath like an unloved christmas decoration. He had taken to cycling to and from work, also, to really exhaust himself, and to get a night's sleep better than what he was getting, what with the stress and the doubting, and the MSG that had invaded his diet, which dehydrated him and woke him in the early hours.

The day after boxing day he had gone to the sales and picked up a clip for his bicycle helmet that allowed him to attach the GoPro. He had done this firstly because the box for the GoPro had listed a number of functions for the camera and he had been disappointed that most of them were not applicable to him or his lifestyle (he did not bungee jump or skydive, or white water raft or climb, and so he had no use for the GoPro in filming him doing these things). He had done this secondly because of the generously dishonest comment he had received from the member of his sister-in-law's family the day before. Specifically, he had decided he would use his GoPro camera to record the dangerous road users he encountered on his commutes. Since he had begun cycling to and from work he had come to realise how inconsiderate British road users were with regards to cyclists. He had not noticed this whilst a driver.

*

On the 22nd of June of that year, Ian Langtree was cycling the Henley road on his way back from work. It was a narrow road at the best of times, and he was cycling a particularly narrow stretch of it, when a blue Ford Transit van - rather than waiting for the oncoming lane to clear - remained in the lane to overtake. The van hurled past him, inches from the cycle, then sped off apparently unfussed. Luckily the whole incident was caught on camera and that evening Ian Langtree uploaded the footage to Youtube with double urgency, sending the link to the Thames Valley Police. Some time passed.

*

At 21 years old Peter Downes was married. Six years later he was divorced, and at 30 he married again. The period between marriages was one of drink abuse, migraines, and a nine-month spell in prison for battery. The advent of his second wife begun a healthier and more stable period of Peter Downe's life. He started his own scaffolding company. He stopped drinking White Ace. The migraines turned into headaches. Now he has two children: Toby Downes from his first marriage and a 6-year-old, Shannon, from his second.

The healthier and more stable period of Peter Downe's life is fast approaching its end. He drinks heavily again, after work, and usually on the sofa alone. And he has progressed from cider to wine, a progression wholly related to the higher alcoholic content of the latter, which he drinks in the same measure. He is also having an affair. Peter Downes is having an affair with an older and more attractive office receptionist, who recently had 'work done to her tits'.

On the 22nd of June of that year, Peter Downes was coming home from work later than usual after stopping off at the older receptionist's flat. He was coming down the Henley road. He did not want to be late because he did not want to encourage the suspicions of his wife, who was always suspicious and not because suspicion was any vice of hers. The traffic was bad. The traffic was not allowing him to get home as quickly as he wanted to, and now a cyclist was in his way. It was a winding part of the Henley road. It would not be possible to overtake for some time; the oncoming lane was busy anyhow. But he did not want to be late and he couldn't be late again, and so he had decided to chance it by remaining within the lane to overtake, albeit staying as much to the right as he could. And he had chanced it well - he considered - because he had overtaken the cyclist easily, and now there was an open stretch of road ahead where he could make up for lost time. That evening his wife's appropriate and valid suspicions were not encouraged.

A month or so later Peter Downes was sat in the on-site portacabin that functioned as his office, sweating out two and a half bottles of Hardy's

9

white wine, and doing his best to make his doing nothing look like some sort of managerial style. For instance, he sighed a lot and leant his chin on his middle and ring fingers, and lay his index finger perpendicular to them along his cheek, like some thinker in an enlightenment era portrait. The large COSTCO tub of instant coffee that was always open (there was never a lid), containing several plastic teaspoons that were never reused, always tipped in tarry bits of re-hydrated instant coffee crystals, sat there goading him, at least he felt. He knew he was feeling peculiar, psychedelic even, and he tried to recall how long it had been now since inanimate objects like a big COSTCO tub of instant coffee had been capable of ruining his day.

He was sitting there, slouched in such a style, muttering to himself alone in the portacabin whilst others put up scaffolds, when one of the boys from the site came in. It was Johnny Croft, son of Alan Croft, who he'd taken on after Alan suffered a stroke on holiday in Spain. Other than that he hated Johnny Croft. He hated him because he thought him a metrosexual. For instance, he spent thirty pounds on haircuts that involved shaving patterns into the side of his head and talked loudly about picking up 'gear' on pay days. Peter Downes called him a "druggy little cunt" as a joke, although there was rarely anything funny in the delivery. Peter Downes hated him because he took drugs that were illegal and he thought that this made him a metrosexual. But Johnny had come to see Peter Downes in his portacabin office because he had something important to show him on his mobile phone, on Youtube.

'Absolute cretin on the Henley road!' Uploaded by LingLang63.

Johnny presses play.

We are watching the events unfold from the perspective of a GoPro camera clipped to the top of a bicycle helmet. A man is cycling along a road. The lane is empty; the oncoming lane is busy. A blue van speeds past. The perspective of the GoPro being unfamiliar, especially when distorted by the incongruent aspect ratio settings inputted by the user, does not give us a useful idea of the van's proximity to the cycle. However, it is implied that the van was close. We understand this first of all from the title (the van driver, we assume, is the cretin), but then from the cyclist who cries out: "Jesus Christ", "Too bloody close", and finally: "R*** ***" (the vehicle's registration number). The video ends with a slow motion replay of the blue Ford Transit van speeding past, and the words 'COMPLETE MORON!' superimposed in size 24 Lucida Console.

Peter Downes, who immediately recognises that it is his van by identification of the number plate, and not from any memory of the incident, wonders how Johnny Croft got to know of the video. He says his mum liked it on Facebook after one of her friends from the Hospice shop shared it. Peter Downes mumbles something about it not being good for business. Then he says something playful to Johnny, like: "well, fuck off out of here, I've got stuff to sort out".
"Are you gonna do anything about it?" asks Johnny.
"Na. I don't giva fuck," Peter Downes replies.

But deep down Peter Downes absolutely does give a fuck. He gives a massive fuck, really, a fuck quite grossly disproportionate to all the other fucks he should be giving right now, including, for instance, a fuck for that as-yet-identified-as-such fatty node on his left testicle. He is livid. So furious, in fact, he thinks his fury a violation of himself. And all he wants to do is grab that twat Johnny's phone from out of his hand and throw it as hard as he can against the portacabin wall, and then catch the bastard and give him a good chinning to teach him for mugging him off like that, especially in *his* office. His rage quite spectacularly deepens, and now he thinks about getting into his van and speeding down the Henley road, knocking every leotard-clad cyclist down like it was a game of skittles, including whatever square-headed nonce uploaded the video of him. Instead, he takes a nap in the portacabin for an hour.

*

Ian Langtree, or LingLang63, logs in to Youtube. He sees he has one new message. He clicks the message to read it.

The message is from Chelseaboyblue117. The message reads:

"Dunno who you think you are but thats my van in your video and you have no rite to put it on the internet. Take it down else i get the police involved"

Ian Langtree is confused. He clicks Chelseaboyblue117's profile and sees the account was created a day ago. Ian Langtree replies:

"What van? I have a lot of videos and a lot of run ins with vans and I can film exactly what I want in a public place, including dangerous and illegal driving."

Ian Langtree waits for an hour, intermittently checking the opened tab for a reply from Chelseaboyblue117. It comes that evening:

"The blue transit. You call me a cretin. Take it down NOW else i get legal action."

Five minutes later, LingLang63 replies:

"Well I have no legal obligation to take my video down. Indeed, it is I who should be seeking legal action in the first place for your ILLEGAL driving."

Up until now, Peter Downes has been relatively tame, civil even, in his proceedings with LingLang63. He has, as you say, 'kept his chill'. And Peter Downes is not a man known for keeping his chill: there are people who have testified that fact. And so it is probably a mixture of LingLang63's stubborn refusal to make any sort of concession with Chelseaboyblue117, not necessarily to remove the video, but at least to attempt some kind of diplomacy which would be a sign to Peter Downes that his macho aggressiveness was being taken seriously, as well as the tone LingLang63 employs which is aggressive in its own kind of inflexible bureaucratic way that in the end causes Chelseaboyblue117 to reply with the following, only forty-five minutes later at 9:37pm on a Tuesday:

"Listen here u little fuckty. Take down ur video else i come to ur house and brake ur gay neck u fucking twat."

To which LingLang63 replies at 9:51pm with:

"I am NOT taking the video down. I am reporting you to the moderators for abusive language and making threats. Your doing nothing right now but demonstrating your propensity for rage that makes you a dangerous driver in the first place".

Chelseaboyblue117 (9:54pm):

"You fucking wat. Speak english. I will find ur address out and then come smash ur fucking house down u little twerp"

LingLang63 (9:58pm):

"How rich, maybe you should learn to spell first."

LingLang63 (10:00pm):

"I highly doubt you are capable of finding my address anyway"

Chelseaboyblue117 (10:07pm):

"I WILL COMe around ur fucking house nd piss on ur things and slap you. Ur testing my fucking patients tonite. Take ur video of me down now else i shove ur camera up ur arse. Im sure u will enjoy it."

Chelseaboyblue117 (10:09pm):

"Yes i can find ur house. Oh wait ur propably homeless and dont have a home…"

LingLang63's report to the youtube moderators has gone through successfully. The Chelseaboyblue117 account is suspended.

*

Peter Downes is not the smartest man around (to say nothing of Ian Langtree). So when he went about setting up his own Youtube channel with the intention of using it to distribute online abuse, he did not think against filling in personal information on his profile, or making it public. For instance, Peter Downes gave his business's website address. On the website, one can find the registered address of the business, which is Peter Downes' home address. How does Ian Langtree know it is Peter Downes' home address? Because he went on Google street view and found the same blue Ford Transit parked in its driveway.

*

13

Ian Langtree has become strange since the divorce. Everyone says it now. And so setting his alarm for 6am the following morning to be outside the front of Peter Downes' house before he has woken up, is a mere extension of these new ways.

It is 8:33 am when Peter Downes and the fat son emerge from their house eating vacuum packed croissants. The croissants were packed several weeks ago in a baked goods factory near Bolton. The fat son carries two full Lidl bags also. Waiting for the blue van to pull out of the drive, Ian Langtree remains hidden behind the lavender bushes, his balding head - the crown shiny and vulnerable looking, stopping abruptly along a contour of frontal bone wherein the scalp becomes matted and hard - protrudes as he watches the vehicle crawl away. It is a delicious blue morning. The dew has already dried. And now Ian Langtree is on his bicycle as he begins to follow the van. Maintaining a distance, he reassures himself he could not be recognised anyway.

He follows Peter Downes in such a way for nearly an hour through the dense rush hour traffic. And now they are out of town and hurling down the Henley road, back in the direction Ian Langtree came that morning. And how queer, Peter Downes takes a left, off the Henley road and back into Twyford.

Ian Langtree is still not sure what he is doing, peddling 20 yards behind Peter Downes' van. He was not sure, either, what he was doing crouched in the bushes of Peter Downes' garden for two hours this morning. Indeed, Ian Langtree is a man who knows some things very well, and other things not at all. His actions since the exchange of messages with Peter Downes the evening before have mostly belonged to this second category of things.

But Ian Langtree knows he knows this: that there is something exhilarating in watching someone and following them, knowing who they are when they cannot know you. There is something thrilling for Ian Langtree who knows he could strike at any moment if he were persuaded. That he could leap out from the sea of anonymity and set upon Peter Downes, like the devil in a cup of Horlicks, some demon in a can of brake fluid; like a monster or phantom or evil hidden in plain sight.

But Ian Langtree is starting to get nervous. The left into Twyford was an amusing coincidence, but now, watching the blue Ford Transit van turn into his little cul-de-sac, Ian Langtree is having a nauseating realisation.

They pull up outside the maisonnette. The fat son hops out. Peter Downes limps. Ian Langtree looks on from across the road, behind a post box.
"We'll have a reccy," says Peter Downes, "See if he's in".
"What if he is in?" asks the fat son.
"I 'ope for blaady 'is sake he ain't," says Peter Downes as if scripted by some working-class fetishist.

Peter Downes presses his face up to the window. He opens the letterbox slot and peeks in. There is no one there. The fat son checks the side of the house, to see if Ian Langtree is in his garden. The fat son crosses the lawn, intentionally eschewing the paving to trample on the easy-grow flowers. Peter Downes tries the doorbell and door knock. Nothing. The fat son returns shaking his head. Peter Downes gives a nod, and the fat son retrieves the Lidl bags from the van. Ian Langtree looks on.

There are eggs in that bag, Ian Langtree can see, and the fat son is careful in opening each crate of twenty-four and distributing them out on the front lawn. Egging the maisonnette, they pay particular attention to the door and windows. Then the fat son has an idea: the two take to aiming exclusively at the ventilation brick of Ian Langtree's bedroom. The idea is that fragments of egg matter will become irretrievably lodged within the insulation gap of the wall resulting in an enduring and festering stench of rotten egg around the home.

Ian Langtree cannot understand it. But what he does not know is that after his conversation with Chelseboyblue117 the evening before, Peter Downes got his son to drive him to Johnny Croft's house in Tilehurst, to wake his mother up at 0:16am asking her for the details of the person who had shared the video of his van on Facebook. Because Peter Downes gave her son a job that helped out the family in the aftermath of her husband's stroke, Peter Downes thinks this sort of behaviour is acceptable and well within his right.

Now, Johnny Croft's mother's friend from the Hospice shop happens to be Ian Langtree's brother's wife, who encourages Ian Langtree's hobby by 'liking' and sharing his videos on Facebook as and when he releases them. Moreover, Ian Langtrec's captions usually involve the personal pronoun

"I". Ian Langtree's faccbook is set to public, and six months ago, after moving to the maisonette in Twyford, he announced the news to Facebook using a Google Maps plugin. This is how Peter Downe's finds out where Ian Langtree lives.

But lo! From out yonder, a war cry? A marauding army? No! Ian Langtree: bursting out onto the cul-de-sac shrieking: "cease this madness!". The last five minutes, climaxing with the chubby son pressing whole eggs into the letterbox slot, have tested the man more than enough.

The next few things happen quickly and are ended by neighbours who appear from houses and pull the two grown men on the lawn apart. The men are up on their feet. Neighbours try to contain them. "Fucking hold me back" wheezes Peter Downes. Ian Langtree's voice keeps breaking as he repeats himself. Order is restored and the neighbours try to piece together the various testimonies as best as they can. But they do not know what is happening, or why. None of them knows what Youtube is, and only one has heard of a GoPro and she thinks it's something for cats. Other things make less sense.

And this is how we end up where we began.

Mark Spriggs, a Durham University educated 48-year-old managing director from the cul-de-sac has an extremely self-confident air about him, verging on the aggressively smug. This is what makes him the good managing director he is, but also, truly unlikable. More than unlikable, even: Mark Spriggs is able to rouse irrational levels of hatred within seconds of meeting. His face, his mannerisms, even his posture is imbued with a smugness that lingers like a tragic death among close family. The only people who like Mark Spriggs are his friends. His friends, and women that are attracted to him. On the latter point, Mark Spriggs does have a chivalrous kind of charm that makes him popular with a certain type of lady. On the former, Mark Spriggs has friends from the airfield. He has sailing friends too. No more than that. Ian Langtree does not like Mark Spriggs because a configuration of a significant number of his attributes activates a subconscious mnemonic fear response in him relating to experiences at grammar school. Mark Spriggs does not like Ian Langtree.

When Mark Spriggs looks out the window and sees the two male adults on the lawn, taking lumps out of one another as a group of terrified neighbours from the cul-de-sac look on, and that one of the two men involved in the grapple, the driver of the parked van, has a large if not lumpy build, and crooked features, and an overall appearance to suggest he is a man who works with his body more than his mind, he realises that the situation provides an opportunity for his taking. Specifically, Mark Spriggs spots this as an opportunity to demonstrate to the neighbours his knack for dealing with situations beyond the confines of the middle-class comfort zone.

"Gentlemen, what are we doing?" booms the approaching Mark Spriggs. Peter Downes (who has since got out of the neighbour's clutches and now sits on Ian Langtree, rubbing his face into the topsoil, repeating "ya facking want somma that?" over and over), recoils on hearing Mark Sprigg's authoritative tone of voice, briefly mistaking Mark Spriggs for a police officer. He rolls off Ian Langtree immediately and quickly gets to his feet.

Breaths are caught, and the men take turns explaining their side of the story. The crowd, which has swollen in size over the last five minutes, watches on like the Roman senate. They umm and ahh in places. They mutter when testimonies contradict. But the 6ft 3, salt and pepper haired Mark Spriggs maintains a diplomatic air throughout. He never gives any indication that he has granted one piece of information more importance than another, or that he believes someone is lying or exaggerating.

But deep down Mark Spriggs has no interest in diplomacy. What Mark Spriggs is really hell bent on is demonstrating to the neighbours his knack for dealing with men's grievances, particularly when these pertain to retrogressive notions of hurt pride and damaged honour and other such matters. Mark Spriggs believes there is something endearing in acknowledging and therefore validating such concerns, especially as they're so seemingly incongruent to the expectations one might have formed of him as an educated, cosmopolitan gentlemen, rather than a man who thinks that two men should 'have it out'.

Mark Spriggs thinks it's awfully charming to do a bit of the old good cop, bad cop. To rough it up a little. Mark Spriggs says: "I get it, when two men have a grievance, they got to settle it" (Mark Sprigg's voice wobbles ever so slightly into tedious cockney here). "It's about pride I get that." What Mark Spriggs pretends he believes is that the two men need to sort out a way of establishing the better man. What Mark Spriggs wants is to demonstrate to the onlookers his knack for dealing with a situation he feels evades the sensibilities of the middle-class onlookers.

What Mark Spriggs does know is that he cannot simply allow the two men to continue taking lumps out of one another. That would not constitute the chivalrous edge he brings to the table. That would not demonstrate to the onlookers - particularly Sally Thompson who has slept with him behind her husband's back for two months now - that he is a man with a knack for dealing with situations that concern men, and the increasingly obsolete undertakings of fighting, avenging and 'settling it once and for all'. To break it down, what Mark Spriggs needs is for the onlookers, particularly Sally Thompson, to think something along the lines of: 'Wow. Where did Mark Spriggs, university educated, former captain of the Durham rugby team, thrice junior sculling champion and managing director of a successful firm (with a robust knowledge of french reds), also find the time to *learn to deal with men*? There must be another side to this great multifaceted personality. He is even more complicated than we first knew. Maybe he was in the army, or spent time in prison, or laboured in docks?'.

"Gentlemen," says Mark Spriggs. "I'm going to let you settle this because I know this is something that needs settling."

There is a roar. Suddenly, everyone remembers they haven't seen the fat son for a while. He comes charging out from behind the van, an 8ft galvanised steel scaffold pole held aloft like a transforming He-Man. But the roar loses its confidence. Quickly it draws to an end, and the fat son's face becomes concentrated as he bounds across the cul-de-sac at Ian Langtree. Onlookers freeze at the unfolding spectacle. The fat son wobbles. His flat soled DC shoes have little traction on the lawn. He wobbles some more. His wobbling has an almost mesmeric quality about it. The fat son loses his footing and loses his grip on the scaffold pole. He slips violently back onto his coccyx, with a crack, not before lashing out at the nothingness in front of him. The scaffold pole, performing a small arch in the air, drops down onto his forehead. The fat son writhes in pain. Big pale shins protruding from beige three-quarter-lengths kick frantically about.

Mark Spriggs has an idea. Before the interruption in the cul-de-sac, he had been watching Knights of the Realm on the UK History Channel. The scaffold pole provides him with his eureka moment. Mark Spriggs knows what to do.

There are some rules and the first rule is that contestants are only allowed one strike. Once someone has been struck the contest is over. If both contestants miss, there is another round. Contestants are not allowed to strike the other using their vehicle. One neighbour speaks up and asks Mark Spriggs if it is rather unfair that Ian Langtree is to lance Peter Downes from a bicycle, whilst Peter Downes gets to lance Ian Langtree from a two-tonne van. Mark Spriggs notes that whilst there is capacity for more severe damage to be incurred on the part of the cyclist, its smaller size and the fact it can be moved quickly (i.e., its higher agility value), means it might avert the other contender more easy, meaning its chance of coming away entirely unscathed is much greater than for the van, which although affords a much higher degree of protection for its contained contender (i.e., its protection value), has a very high chance of sustaining at least some damage (a shattered windscreen, a broken wing mirror, etc). "It's simple probability consequentialism," says Mark Spriggs with a knowing look.

The fat son sits out for the joust. He is tended to by Mal White's daughter-in-law for his nasty head injury.

The van faces the bicycle. The bicycle faces the van. Mark Spriggs wets his lips, then counts the two men in. He hopes that in less than a minute he will be able to demonstrate to the onlookers his knack, not only for first-aid, but also for remaining level-headed in an emergency situation, and dealing confidently and appropriately with the authorities.

Peter Downes' lance rests out of the side window. The lance is an 8ft galvanised steel scaffold pole from his van. He will push it forward and out of the vehicle at Ian Langtree's head or chest when he thinks the timing is right. Ian Langtree rests his lance on the handlebar. He steers the bicycle with his left hand.

Peter Downes' van is accelerating. Ian Langtree has reached his top speed of 13mph. The two vehicles are approaching. Ian Langtree thinks now is the time to defer speed for accuracy. He decelerates, slightly, to 11mph. He levels the scaffold pole out. The van reaches 30 mph. He thinks of Emily in her Cotswold stone cottage. The crowd craves quietly an outcome it knows it should not want.

The van is at 36 miles an hour, and the bicycle at 10, when first contact is made. The contact is made between the end of Ian Langtree's scaffold pole and the windscreen of Peter Downes' blue Ford Transit. The windscreen shatters in a millisecond, producing a stained glass effect. Instantly, Peter Downes is unable to see anything. He lashes out with his scaffold pole. Before he can hope to have struck Ian Langtree, he feels his breathing stop. An agonising pain erupts from his throat box. "A scaffold pole collapsed your windpipe," he will later be told.

Peter Downes is tended to on the lawn by Mark Spriggs, who tells the hysterical Sally Thompson, firmly and calmly, that she must phone for an ambulance. Peter Downes spits out globules of blood. Two men from the cul-de-sac reverse the crumpled up van out of Mal White's flower beds. "She'll be devastated when she gets home", her daughter-in-law says. The fat son's forehead is better now and the boy cries at the side of his father who phlegms gurgled obscenities through the thick fluid building up in his brutalised trachea.

Ian Langtree is confused about how he should feel, although he thinks it was probably a good thing he ducked when he did. Mark Spriggs explains that he will most likely be arrested. Mark Spriggs warns him not to say anything until he has his lawyer. Mark Spriggs reassures him he knows a decent lawyer, his card he has somewhere.

Ian Langtree does not know what to do as he waits, perched on the cul-de-sac pavement. He knows he can go into his house, but he doesn't think it appropriate. Instead, he stays put on the roadside whilst neighbours rush around Peter Downes, lying back like a starfish, as blood and mucus eject from him, who gnashes unholy things at not just Ian Langtree but the angels trying to help him. He sits on the kerb and wonders if he should phone Emily, but figures she will find out soon anyway. And how much better the whole thing will sound if it comes from someone else's mouth. Anyway, he unclips the GoPro from his bicycle helmet and stops the thing recording.

Nightmares

He's alone in the office when the phone rings. "Leonardo's fine dining, how can we help?" he answers hesitantly, pausing a hentai.

Static. *Cuuurrrgh.* Then: "Is shish Baafffy?" - a bark from the noise. In grating faux cockney - mockney - subconsciously met with: "h-hoo's askin'?".

Static, or breathing? And now he thinks breathing. The rasp of a kazoo, or, *an electrolarynx.* It couldn't be. It's not-

"Ish Bill," the voice from the noise again. "You remember ol' Bill, dontchu?"

"Bill?" his voice wobbles. "Co'rse I do," the mockney contagious. And now he's sweating, a cold sweat exuded from everywhere.

"Atta boy, I knew you would. Naa Baaffy, I got somin' for ya. A project ya mart like." And Buffy is listening: "I'm all ears, Bill".

And Bill explains he'd like to get Leonardo's on the show. That this would be the end, of course, it always is. "I'm retiring you boy, be 'appy baat it. Goda Spain or somefin'. Shoak up shum shun."

And Buffy, no choice but to say: "Thanks, Bill," and thinks, at least this saves an insurance job.

"Sending some boys ova' tomorrow morning," says Bill. "Forra nosey. You'll be there."

"I'll-" *Cuuuuurrrrrrrggggghhhhh.* The line goes dead.

*

Abel Abboud is a 22-year-old pot wash at Leonardo's restaurant. Born in the Darfur region of Sudan, he fled his war-torn town as a teenager, heading north to Libya alone by foot. After a brief spell in Ajdebya, Abel crossed the Mediterranean sea via canal barge alongside 3000 other refugees. The trip cost him his savings and nearly his life. He was pulled from the sea by the Italian navy and sent to the Lampedusa immigration reception centre in Southern Italy. After his escape, he settled in the Calais

"Jungle" camp in France. He applied for French asylum twice, but heard nothing back. In the camp, they said he'd be deported. He decided to try for Britain instead.

One evening at a Calais ring road, Abel broke into a moving meat lorry and hid under a stack of vacuum-packed chicken giblets. Border patrol laughed when the lorry set the dogs off. For six hours he remained submerged under giblets, until the lorry reached a nugget factory in Neath, Wales. At the nugget factory the driver let Abel go through the fire exit. From Neath, he walked north-eastwards until he reached the Brecon Beacons national park. He survived on rabbit and wild fruit. In Crickhowell, two dog walkers pointed him towards Cardiff, and so he made his way to the city through the beautifully grazed valleys of the Welsh countryside. In Cardiff, he was arrested and put in immigration detention. He spent several months in a detention centre before it was shut down by the Home Office following reports of 'human rights misconduct'. Abel was moved somewhere else, where he spent more time. With the help of voluntary legal professionals, he was eventually granted asylum and put in temporary housing in Bristol. He's getting on with his life now: training part-time as an accountant, seeing a specialist. The nightmares haven't gone, mind. And in some way, of course, he still misses Sudan.

Buffy is the owner of Leonardo's, although Buffy is not his real name, and no one knows how old he is. For three years his restaurant has received the informal accolade of the worst in Bristol. Several Tripadvisor reviews refer to the full-scale Teenage Mutant Ninja Turtle statue in the dining room as tacky and incoherent. In an article from 2013, the Bristol Post referred to the statue as: "a prognostication, or perhaps, comment on, the impending experience". Buffy thinks it sublime. Despite voting UKIP for explicitly anti-immigration reasons, Leonardo's has avoided bankruptcy on several occasions due to the illegal exploitation of its immigrant workforce. Sometimes, when talking to diners, Buffy will use phrases commonly invoked by people for whom English is their second language. For instance, he might break his speech up with a winced: "eh, how you say?", performing a stereotypically latin hand gesture (rotating wrist. Pinched thumb and index finger). But English is his first language; there is no second. He's never even been to Italy.

*

Nine o' clock Wednesday morning and the men from the show arrive. They park their large saloon car across the yellow dividing lines and brake hard so that it smells of burning. "We're Bill's boys," says a man in a fedora, offering Buffy a handshake. Buffy thinks they look like budget TV gangsters; a confused mismatch of various mobster tropes. "Pleasure," he says, taking the hand, eyeing greedily the black duffle bag in the other. "Welcome to the dungeon." They descend into Leonardo's.

Half an hour later and the men file out. Buffy, following last, looks pleased. "Perfect," growls the old one in the Sicilian Coppola. He reaches into his coat pocket for a tin of cigarillos. The young one does his light. "Blaady perfect. A right shit 'ole; true pig sty."
"Thanks," says Buffy.
"Bill'll be proper 'appy," the old man says. "TV crew'll be rand next week to crack on. Allie boy," he snaps his fingers - the man in the fedora hands him the duffle bag. "Ish for you," the old man says, throwing the bag to the ground. "S'all there." Then the men pile back into the car and are gone as quickly as they came. The smell of stale tobacco and burnt rubber lingers in the air. Buffy spends the afternoon on Autotrader.

*

The following Monday the TV crew arrives; Leonardo's is closed for three days.

*

Thursday, and Leonardo's looks different. Not just the crew and TV equipment all over, but also, an enhanced grubbiness than before. Fresh grease stains dirty kitchen surfaces; anonymous liquid collects lethally in depressions on the tiled floor; decomposing food decorates the room with an ornate, almost purposeful quality. *Sabotage.* Or was it always this way? And Buffy has changed. No longer packed in a rip-off silk shirt, he hangs out a grubby vest. Recently removed jewellery reveals white lines across his pink knuckles. Where he's usually clean shaven, angry black and white stubble sprouts from his loveless jowls. Fidgety, *sober* - something is wrong.

And the chefs are gone, or rather, they haven't shown up. "One fucking day and those cunts let me down," says Buffy, downing the ends of a Red Bull. "They can kiss their cut bye-bye."

The TV producer tells Buffy: "Get something sorted, he's here in five".
Five, then: "He's here!".
"He's here!" the runners and waiters bleat.

Gordon Ramsay enters the room to the applause of the Leonardo's staff. Abel Abboud does not know who this is. He thinks he recognises the face from the TV, or perhaps, a magazine he flicked through in the centre. It certainly has its distinguishing features. And now he thinks, surely, he has seen the face somewhere. Where exactly eats at him until the feeling subsides, and now he thinks it's simply one of those faces that creates an illusion of recognition. Some universality in those features. "Feckin' clap," growls Buffy through gritted teeth. Abel claps with the others who whistle

and cheer the man's entrance.

The big man smokes a vape pen the size of a walkie-talkie and sips coffee from a novelty-sized thermos mug. A big novelty-sized thermos mug. The sort of novelty-sized thermos mug ordered from the States that takes three weeks for its delivery. The kind of novelty-sized thermos mug thats decadence upsets the elderly. And he's really going for the coffee. *Glugluglug* followed by huffs on the vape pen. Big huffs, like he was drinking from it, thick milkshake. And Buffy holds out his hand, says: "Welcome to Leonardo's," met with a look of revulsion by the big man. Revulsion turns to fury, as the big man's face reddens. A quiver of the lip; pangs of hatred manifest as flashes of migrainic white light in his skull, then deep breaths - back to calm. The big man's face folds into a half-smile, he jokes: "Hands are busy. Tug me off?", and Buffy laughs, miming the proposed gesture. But the big man is on to someplace else: scolding a runner for slouching!

Chitter chatter and nervous excitement, like a rained-off playtime, as waiters wrestle for autographs, and the techies set up lights. Reproaching

Buffy, the producer says: "get something sorted now". Buffy has an idea.

"Abdul!"
"Abel,"
"Abel?"
"That's Abdul," says Abel, pointing to the Bangladeshi porter.
"Abel. I'm teasing."
"..."
"Abel," he says, his arm around Abel, his voice lowered. "What would you say if I made you chef for the day?".
"I can't cook," Abel shrugs.
"Nonsense," says Buffy. "Course you can." Then he wrestles something out from underneath the sink. "It's easy. Just a case of following these," he says handing Abel a stack of filthy laminated sheets. Laminated sheets detailing prep for the 100+ items on the Leonardo's menu. And now, less friendly: "You're gonna be chef for the day; you're gonna pretend you always was".
"Boss, am I going to be on TV?" asks Abel. But the laminated sheets are tucked well into his arms now, and Buffy is off to tell the producer the

good news.

"Positions everybody!"

Pete is a 19-year-old runner for the TV company. Pete has NVQs in sound engineering. Pete wants to be a techie, but for now he's a runner. When one of the real techies is setting up a light, or a microphone, or some such piece of television equipment, Pete will ask the techie a question about that piece of equipment. He will ask a very technical question, presupposing a great deal of technological knowledge on his part, sometimes providing two possible solutions to the problem to imply that technology is not an open-ended mystery to him. Other times he will cut the techie's response short with the correct answer, suffixing this with a: "Yeah, na, I thought so".

"He's gonna need these from the menu," says Pete, handing Abel a list. "Get cooking." Then: "Kapish?" says Pete, snapping his fingers. "You there?", he says, waving a hand in front of Abel, snapping his fingers again. "You there? Kapish?".

The snaps of Pete's fingers have become the snaps of twigs breaking in a daydream. Hiding in grass: Abel hides from men who look for him, who hear broken twigs. If he does not want to be found, he knows he cannot break any more twigs. But in this grass dugout, it all feels like a game. The stakes are higher, of course - he'll be more than 'it' if he's found - but the rush is no different, no greater, than those games as a child. We have to do more to feel the same, he thinks. "Abel" the men cry. Dangerous men with guns. "Abel". If they find you they'll kill you. "Abel-"

"Abel, you dozy twat!" He's back in the room. Buffy in his face. "He's talking to you, you ditzy plonk."
"Here, get cooking pal," says Pete, handing Abel the order.
"Yeah, get cooking," says Buffy.
"Sorry boss," says Abel.
"You will be," says Buffy, exchanging a knowing nod with Pete. A nod of practical men. A nod affirming mutual disdain of their abnormal.

He's alone in the kitchen whilst other things happen in the dining room, and in the kitchen from the dining room, he can hear the intermittent cries of "action!" and "cut!". A noise of bassy grumbles also, occasionally evolving into something more audible. Although the quantity of items on the menu card is at first intimidating (including even 'Indian' and 'Chinese' sections), he notices that many dishes are simple repeats, save for minor alterations to toppings or some such superficial ingredient. For instance, a cheese and tomato pizza topped with chunks of spiced chicken becomes the 'leaning tower of pizza' - the terracotta coloured pieces of cuboidal chicken meat representing scattered bricks (imagining the fall of *the* tower). However, substitute the spiced chicken pieces with prawns, on the same cheese and tomato pizza, and you have 'Pompeii 2': the curled up crustaceans, cooked pink, representing victims of the first great tragedy.

Buffy enters the kitchen. "One more fucking day," he says to himself, combing at his hair, his lip gurning in agitation. "I'll give you fucking à la carte." He phlegms into the sink, which he tries to wash down with the tap but finds it's out of the water's radius. "I'll show you our hygiene score." The whirl of running water only teases the edge of the yellow discharge, which he's forced to coax down the plughole with his finger. Then he's over to Abel.

"What's this then?" asks Buffy, an arm around Abel's shoulder.
"Robert De Niro pizza, sir."
"Robert De Niro Pizza?"
"Yes, sir."
Buffy nods. "Well smack some of this on it," he says, retrieving a jar of Bovril from the fridge and spreading it across the pizza base. "And this?" he asks, inspecting a mixing bowl."That's cheese mix, boss," says Abel. "For the Mussolini Macaroni."
"Right," says Buffy, charging back to the fridge for a Munch Bunch. "We'll give it its namesake," he says pouring the strawberry yoghurt into the bowl.

The dishes are finished and taken through to the dining room. Abel looks on from the kitchen, through the small porthole in the door. He can see the big man at the table, the camera filming him whilst he eats. The man picks at the dishes with his hands, discards pieces of meal onto the floor; whoops, occasionally, random obscenities.

Pete enters the kitchen. "In five he's going to want to see you. Let him talk first, okay, even if he's shouting. Now, the key-phrase is: 'The cheese was so plentiful, it could have given me a heart attack'. That's your cue.

That's when you go for it. That's when you give him hell. It's important you do. Rockets need resistance to fly. Not too hard, mind, and keep the swearing down. We don't wanna bleep the whole bleedin' thing out. You got it? Good." Gordon Ramsay bursts into the kitchen holding handfuls of his dinner, with cheese around his chin. The cameras follow. A crowd gathers.

"Hello, Hello," says Gordon Ramsay, bouncing from foot to foot. "Can I speak to the chef?".

"That's me, sir," says Abel.

"Fuck me," says Gordon Ramsay, his eyes scanning the kitchen. "So you cooked me this shit show of shite?", he says, the alliteration causing him to salivate at the edges of his mouth. "That was a fucking disgrace." He holds up a slice of the Robert De Niro pizza, scrunching it up in his hand like tissue paper. A piece of pastrami meat squeezes through the gaps of his fingers and gently descends down a strand of processed cheese like a spider along its web. They watch it fall together. There is pastrami in the Robert De Niro pizza because pastrami is popular in New York, as well as with taxi drivers, and Taxi Driver, which Robert De Niro starred in.

"Robert De Niro pizza?" asks Gordon Ramsay, his bouncing from foot-to-foot faster now. "What the fuck were you on?" Then he laughs, a sinister laugh, to himself, like a young girl's. "He told me there's Bovril in it," he says, pointing to Buffy, mouthing "Bovril" again with emphatic disgust. "Wouldn't feed Bovril to my rats." Then from his left cheek, he removes a frankfurter. A tinned frankfurter with the tip inserted in a hollowed-out habanero pepper. An hors d'oeuvre listed as: 'Michelangelo's paintbrush'. He removes the starter halfway from his mouth, the protruding bit wobbling as he talks. "Muchansshhelo's panbrusssh?" he says, his eyes fixed on Abel all the while. "Loosh lark Muchansshhelo's cock tuh me". And now he is nearer, tugging the frankfurter to the side of his mouth. "Loosh like Michelanshelo's shaft and knob cap". Then with a hacking cough, he expels the hors d'oeuvre onto the floor. Sputum-coated like an amniotic sack, the phlegmy starter slaps the kitchen tiles with a squelch. Which reminds listeners of their flesh. The dark moistness of insides.

"Looks like Michelangelo stuck his big renaissance willy in a pepper, and fucked it".

And Abel tries to look down at the semi-regurgitated starter on the floor but Gordon Ramsay's head follows his line of sight, filling his field of vision.

"You're not a fucking chef. You're a cunt".

Then Gordon Ramsay is over at the cupboards, searching for things. His tongue flaps around the edge of his mouth with the urgent movements of a suffocating fish. "Well fuck me," he says, removing a jar of whelks from the shelf. "Four years off their sell-by-date: are you trying to kill someone?", then, "Jesus": a rotting cucumber wrapped in tissue paper.

"Cripes," he says, pulling a rusty razor blade from an apple.
Then a runner wheels in a trolley through a gap in the crowd. On the trolley is a casserole dish of Mussolini Macaroni. "Bet you wish you'd seen the last of me," says Gordon Ramsay from the side of his mouth,

33

ventriloquising the cheesy main course. "Bet you wish he'd gobbled me all up". And Gordon Ramsay circles the trolley, stares the macaroni down. Removing a little fork from his breast pocket, he crouches down to the level of the trolley, breathing heavily through his nostrils. With the fork he breaks the golden seal of the macaroni, tearing away a piece of the pasta tethered by strands of stringy cheese. He chews the mouthful with a concentration bordering on the facetious, and swallows with a pronounced gulp. Then he wretches and is sick all over the floor.

The crowd looks on.

Gordon Ramsay gets up and gets right in Abel's face. Close, so that Abel can smell his aftershave and, he thinks, his wife's *eau de toilette*. And Gordon Ramsay stares straight into Abel's eyes, readjusting his scrotum through his trousers as he does. "The cheese," whispers Gordon Ramsay, nearly inaudible, elongating the '-se'. "The cheese was so plentiful" - now, nearer - "that" - and Abel cannot help but noticing the man's face: how the skin sags and swells, how lines form and go like waves or shapes in clouds - "it could have given me a fucking heart attack". He arcs the "-eart'" and "-ttack" to create a half-rhyme. Veins protrude around his neck and in the spaces, flesh recedes.
There is silence as the crowd watches on in violent anticipation. "Give him hell," mouths Pete. But Abel's face is expressionless. He rubs his eyes. To elsewhere. An expanse of rust-coloured earth, cut by the blue of sky. In the distance he watches children play. They run and shout; he rubs his eyes again to see clearer. There is urgency in those screams; no playfulness in that run. Children don't run in straight lines unless they have to. Smog is acrid and burns his nostrils, stings his eyes. He rubs some more. *Ktktktktktktkt.* The snap, crackle and pop of the machine gun. Real screams. Close your eyes. Rub them, it feels good. Then he's back in the room; back with the man. "Don't cry, boy," the man says, his head gyrating about his neck. "I'll give you something to cry about."

"Boss." Abel exhales, looking to the crowd for help.

"I said, are ya tryna gizus a FOOCKIN' ART TARK WITH THUS CHAZE!", the man booms, the flesh on its face amorphous as form recedes.

"EUKAN ARTARK!" bursts from a flap, spraying throat debris. Throat debris that smells of damp silage. "AT NAK, AT NAK, AT NAK!" it howls, in seeming discomfort, the face folding in on itself, resembling, now, a flannel. And where there were previously features, pink folds of skin envelop the last traces of humanity.

Then it sings. Or rather, singing starts, because it is not clear how the thing in the room could produce the sounds, especially in their plurality. Baritone, soprano and tenor. A crescendo in sopranino. Face folds quiver in coterminal frequency. Then it becomes four as if seen through a kaleidoscope, and the four are under a spotlight, like in Queen's *Bohemian Rhapsody*.

"NAAAAAK" in G, tenor, the top one.

"AAARKKK" a C, the sopranino, the left one.

And so on. And now he is everywhere. And he has been everywhere. And he is everything. In some way he always was.

35

5

4

3

2

1

Some of the runners said they heard it and that it sounded like the noise a stapler makes. *Ftuck*. Then his face is released from its ghastly oppression and Gordon Ramsay is returned to the room, albeit with the features of a younger self. And for a moment he sways on two feet, coming to terms with it all like he's just woken from a thousand year dream. In the dark reflection of Bovril, stuck to the end of a kitchen knife, he watches the entirety of his life play out before him.

And in that moment he gets it. He gets it all. It's Leonardo. Of course, it fucking is. It's Leonardo from Teenage Mutant Ninja Turtles. *Hence*. It's sublime. It's beautiful, it's all just a joke.

"Haha.
"Hahahahahahahahahahahahahahahahahahahahahah" he shrieks, and pisses himself.
Then, shock across his boyish face as he stomachs the consequences of all things, Gordon Ramsay falls to the floor with a clump. Cannelloni stored in his breast pocket squelches as he does. The red of the tomato sauce against his chef whites looks like fake blood. A gunshot to the heart in a budget gangster show. And Pete on his chest, pumping away. It all makes sense. It all makes so much sense.
"

The Spontaneous Castration
of Adam Price

When Adam Price came around on his bedroom floor after what might have been seconds or even days, he found that he no longer had any genitals. And where there had been a set of functioning genitals some moments earlier, there was now skin: unblemished skin so that his crotch resembled a stripped Action Man's. Stumbling around the room in a daze, he discovered a penis in the desk drawer. His penis, he suspected, because it looked like his penis, with its shape and its colour and the birthmark near the root. Other things being equal, the only difference Adam Price could make out between the penis in the drawer and the one that had been attached to his crotch only seconds or maybe hours earlier, was the size. The penis had grown: to the size of an arm, in fact. And it seemed amused by having done so in such a bastard manner, Adam Price felt, because the foreskin had shrivelled so as to resemble some beastly grin. A smirk, which the longer he stared at, the more it seemed to grow, eventually enveloping the 'face' and reforming as something new, akin to knowing smugness.

First, he touched it with a pen. He poked a *Premier Inn Hotels* pen into the side to ensure it wasn't filled with cream or piñata innards because part of him still held onto the possibility it was all a joke. A peculiar thing happened when he poked the penis. That is, he felt the poke. He felt the nib of the pen going into its side, and he felt this localised to the space a foot or so below his crotch. He poked it again and he poked it in varying places along the shaft and glans, and he felt, each time, the nib prodding the respective location between his legs as if it were part of him. Then he picked it up. And he felt too, hands - his hands - holding the penis. And now he was more interested in the thing's physicality, than the strange sensations between his legs. The back of the penis, that is, where the penis would otherwise have been attached to him, was as smooth and tight as the new skin around his crotch. The thing had a pulse, too. Though it was heavy to hold being almost three foot long and it strained his arm, and so he put the thing down on the desk to better think about everything that had happened and what it could all mean.

His next idea was that the whole situation might be more easily resolvable with a cup of tea. He dressed (he had been naked when he'd come to) and, anxious that one of his roommates might see the thing, he tried to put it back in the desk drawer he'd found it. But getting it back in was a challenge in itself. Compasses and various protractor shrapnel threatened to prod and splinter his sensitive areas. He settled for under the duvet as a hiding place. "I'll be back for you," he told the thing firmly, squidging its foreskin in such a way for it to resemble something more (suitably) downcast. "That's better," he said, leaving his bedroom cautiously and checking the hallway to ensure he had not been heard.

Whilst waiting for the kettle to boil, Adam Price felt an erotic sensation overcome him. A pleasant tingling from the crotch lasting several seconds, followed by excruciating pain in the same place as if someone were stabbing his genitals with scissors. He screamed and fell to the floor, and held himself tightly down there. And he howled and hissed like an old steam train, in agony. Next, he felt wishing. A *whish whishing* feeling. And it reminded him of summer days: sticking a hand out the car window and feeling warm air trickle between his fingers. Next, the pain again. In double measure. And this time he could taste blood in his throat, so intense it was. "The penis!" he shrieked. "My penis!". And he darted to his bedroom up the stairs, wincing and moaning and buckling to the floor as he made his way - springing back to his feet each time with new urgency.

In the bedroom he found Spuddy the house dog ravaging his organ like it were slaughterhouse offal. "Shoo! Shoo!" he shrieked and waved his arms. But Spuddy paid no attention to the gesticulations. He tried wrestling the penis from the border terrier's mouth but that only encouraged it further.

Smack. It whimpered and scurried out. Inspecting the damage, he was relieved to see most of it was superficial. There were slight puncture wounds from the teeth and a coating of saliva. He cleaned the thing with a wet wipe and applied Savlon to the bite marks. Afterwards, he put the penis in a carrier bag and double knotted it to be sure.

The thread had since been deleted and the forum was silent on the matter. The phone number didn't work so he mistrusted the email. "Hunter_101's Penis Enlargement" returned nothing on Google. He crawled onto the bed and read again with fresh application the leaflet that had come with the pill. He'd done all the stretches correctly, he was sure, and he couldn't see how he fitted any of the 'Not suitable for' criteria. Maybe the pill had been a dud. A factory reject. NO RETURNS. He typed into the 'New Thread' box: "Hunter_101's Penis Enlargement - Feedback Thread". "A thread for customers to give feedback and discuss their experience with Hunter_101's penis enlargement treatment." He clicked 'POST' and waited. He refreshed the page after a few minutes. Then, deciding to get the ball rolling himself, he wrote: "So far, so good. Day one and I can see some progress. Easy to follow instructions. Only downsides: pill made me a bit groggy. Still, great value for $9.99. Thank you, Hunter!".

Five minutes later and his was the top thread in the forum. The replies had come in their droves. Sickboy1337 had said: "All i can say is that i'm best pleased *thumbs up emoji**winkey face emoji*. Will keep you guys updated with further developments!". And Harry_The_Honey had posted: "It's huge! Fantastic value". Dafney^theKID said: "Too big. Girlfriend left me. Very happy". But nothing, absolutely nothing on spontaneous castration. Then again, who'd admit that on the internet, Adam Price thought?

By the time he'd given up on the forum, he was onto his third mug of tea, and was beginning to feel discomfort somewhere around his abdomen. A tenderness at his lower belly, accompanied by an increasing sense of urgency. The penis, he thought. It had to be the penis. And he unknotted the M&S bag and saw that the penis was fine, if not a little sweaty. Airing it out of the bag, the sense of urgency didn't go away. Indeed, he was beginning to feel panic coming over him. Dread, as the feeling evolved into something more physical. "Urghhhhh," he groaned. And he groaned until the feeling reached a climax and then, all of a sudden, *relief.* The blissful release of... pain. And... the penis! Which was flowing! Pissing jets about the bedroom floor. And the idea hadn't yet crossed his mind, that beyond an overlapping nervous system, the thing and he might share... *a bladder*. And so he squeezed his all of a sudden familiar bladder muscle and stopped the flow, and scooped the member back up into the bag and dashed to the toilet. Holding the thing above the toilet bowl to relieve himself, he thought how big things seemed little next to the big things happening to him that day. And for a moment the absurdity of it all prompted laughter from Adam Price that quickly turned into crying, which lasted that way for the best part of an hour.

Naturally, he told no one. But as the days and weeks went by, Adam Price felt he was developing a resilience to the whole situation. His habits were changing: he spent less time online and more outside. He went on walks and talked to strangers. He did not feel so scared. And each time he went on his walks he took with him the penis rolled up into a knock-off Emporio Armani satchel bag. He took it with him because he didn't trust leaving the thing at home with his housemates who might find it, or Spuddy the house dog, sniffing it out for round two. Also, he took it with him because he liked to have it near him. When it was about his person, in the knock-off Emporio Armani satchel bag, it felt as if it was his. Not just his penis, but his big penis. His big penis the size of an arm.

Once some weeks had passed and the adrenaline provoked by the situation had subsided, other chemicals began to factor in and influence events in new ways. One day something embarrassing happened. Adam Price had boarded the number 26 bus on his way to feed the ducks when all of a sudden thoughts about tits and asses crossed his mind, and he could feel the eroticness of his thinking transfer into something more... real. Which was a 'hard on'. He hadn't yet seen the penis get that way since the event. And now, having entertained thoughts about tits and asses, quite automatically and for some time, his mind flashed to the contents of his bag, which he beheld on the seat next to him, near fit to bursting. A young boy opposite said: "the man's bag - it's growing!". And he was so freaked by the possibility of discovery that the erotic quality of his thoughts instantly subsided, and he was relieved to hear the young boy remark: "now it's shrinking!". He got off the bus and ran home and went straight to his bedroom, bolting the door shut with a bolt he'd recently fitted.

Not only was he curious but now he felt he had an obligation to see to it that such events weren't repeated. The first time, naturally, was the strangest, but after that, it got markedly more normal. *It's my penis,* he told himself. *I'm doing this to me like any other person would. It's just that there's space between me. My penis is like Alaska to the Union.* It didn't take long for Adam Price to imagine what else he could do with his new arrangement. Self-fellatio, according to the forums, was a good thing. He remembered Mickey's thread that suggested if all men could, there'd be no need for women. And so he self-fellated and masturbated for reasons of both biological impulse and pragmatism.

One day whilst getting off the number 26 bus, Adam Price was mugged of his satchel bag in broad daylight. The thief ran off before he was able to react, and he stood there, rooted to the pavement in shock. For although the penis had left him, he had not left the penis, and he could still sense its movements: jerking about in the bag as the thief sprinted away.

After five minutes (having taken a seat in a nearby cafe to calm down and better concentrate), he could feel the penis settle into a gentle bob. It bobbed along for half an hour in such a way, until he felt it straddling a lap. A cold breeze against his skin, then *phdud*: "Ouch", and now he felt it on damp leaves, exposed to the chilly autumnal afternoon. He took a bus home. Over dinner, he felt whiskers and a wet nose down there. Thankfully less interested than Spuddy, he thought. After dinner, he watched a movie. *Minions.* Then he went to bed. Sometime in the middle of the night he woke to his penis being lifted and carried away by two pairs of hands and rolled into what felt like a polythene sheet. Then, soft rumbling. What he suspected was a car engine. And he felt it rumble through the night until he was once again dreaming.

In the morning, the rumbling stopped and he could feel the penis placed in packaging material. For the next few days it sat motionless. Slowly, the parcel became soaked in his urine, causing the skin to irritate. It was eventually taken out, washed and repackaged. Sometime that afternoon, he felt the penis begin to gently rock. It took a few days for him to realise it was at sea. Two weeks went by. Over burgers, the rocking stopped. That evening it accelerated to hundreds of miles an hour then underwent g-force. The landing was bumpy, he could tell. More manhandling. Then nothing. Senselessness. He checked his crotch every morning for the next few weeks. Always the same, always bare; no feeling from the penis, wherever it might be.

Six months passed, and life went on. Adam Price rarely thought about the penis anymore. Where it was, whether it would return. The questions seldom occupied his thoughts as deep down he'd come to believe he was no longer intertwined with it. That its effects had worn off, or he was no longer in range of its feeling. Part of him even questioned his recollection of events and wondered if it wasn't all a figment of his imagination: an escape from the real details of some barbaric dismemberment that had happened to him. But because he hadn't told anyone, he couldn't verify beyond himself, what he understood to be the case. And after months of such panics, they now occurred with reduced regularity and intensity. He was nearly fine. The human spirit was a resilient thing.

But then one day Adam Price felt something that startled him. He felt, down there: *phhslapp*. It felt like his penis keeling over and hitting some hard surface with the mass it had. And now he could feel himself against a textured surface. Something bumpy that itched the sides of him. He felt this for the next few days, as the bumpiness irritated him more and more. And it was not just the itchiness that annoyed him, but the reintroduction of feeling down there, which reinvigorated his mind with questions that cluttered his brain and drew him back to the same places.

One evening he sat at his desk and endeavoured to draw out what he was feeling. It was only a hunch, but Adam Price sensed a meaning to the little bumps. Straining to concentrate, he drew the dots out where he felt them. *Pit pit pit*, - he went at the paper with his pen. And as he did his heart beat faster. For his hunch was proving correct: there was not randomness to the dots, but order! They formed patterns that implied language. *Braille.* Could it be that his penis was rested on a braille code? He laughed out loud at the idea, and laughed for some time. But once he had expunged all desire to do so, he got to work, studiously copying the dotted pattern that he felt.

By the time he'd finished it was five in the morning and outside the bedroom window he could hear birds becoming restless in the trees and the familiar tinkling of a milk float. Before him were several sheets of paper, mostly scribbles, containing the occasional gems of code he'd spent hours copying. Torrenting some braille translation software - *BrailleLate*

44

-, he inputted the code by clicking dots with his mouse. The nerves didn't hit him until right at the end, as he finished the last letters. *Here goes.* 'Translate'.

BrailleLate detects your input code is Braille Mandarin Chinese. YES or NO?

Mandarin Chinese. *Shit.* And he had no option but to click, YES.

Select Output Code.

He scrolled through the list of languages and selected: English (British).

BrailleLate is translating your message. Please be patient.

And then.

"Possibly a pre-Cambrian plant form or, as suggested by Dr Yan, perhaps extra-terrestrial, the 'spitting elephant's trunk' is currently the most exciting exhibit at the Nantong Museum. Donated by a patron of the-."

He read it five times before he typed 'Nantong Museum' into Google. Nantong natural history museum. Nantong, China. He smirked as it begun to dawn on him. Click. He entered the website. Click: 'Current Exhibits', and now he was giddy. And in current exhibits: 'The Spitting Elephant's Trunk'. He laughed out loud. And within a few short seconds he was in hysterics: snorting and weeping at the sight on his computer screen. The sight of his penis, suspended in a large glass display, decorated by plastic foliage and papier-mache rocks. A prehistoric plant or an alien: The Spitting Elephant's Trunk! He giggled and hooted until his belly hurt, and then roared with his throat until that hurt too.

Before he fainted and collapsed to the floor, and crawled to the toilet to be sick a number of times, he read the text below the image that Chrome had automatically translated. *"For purposes of scientific enquiry, we will perform a public dissection on the Spitting Elephant's Trunk on the afternoon of the 18th".* He checked the date. The 17th. The next flight to Nantong was £4000.

The Thanet Chess Club Revolution, or
How We Saved the World.

To think the only fairy tale of our history was one of murder. Love never did rescue the suffering prince!

It was a pervasive fear of death that had led to the problems of the societies of America and Europe, but it was death that eventually provided the freedom from the chains to which the people were in bondage. It was not fear of death in death's more banal sense either (diabetes, traffic accidents, and so on.), but rather death in the causally efficacious sense (manifestly efficacious: i.e., obvious to the weak human intellect that sees so little as linked, for everything is causal) - i.e. murder, and murder most foul, which is what this story is about.

It was murder the people feared - being murdered - and not sugar or speed, and it was not some timely, convenient set of deaths that provided the redemption I have been vague about, which I appreciate the reader is eager to discover. It was murder - murder and the Thanet Chess Club - that helped the people achieve the freedom which in the end the whole world would enjoy, live happily ever after, forever and ever, Amen.

*

Our story begins in a nursing home outside of Thanet, where plot is brewing. Brewing like a steaming hot cup of PG tips. Then it moves on, quickly, to several locations around the land of Great Britain, where on the morning of the 1st of November 2031 seven corpses have been discovered. Dead from seven different causes, but causes all united under the term: *murder!*

Back to the nursing home, and there are seven arrests and seven confessions from seven returning patients. Margaret had been away 'visiting family', but returns at lunchtime on the 1st, asks for a telephone and requests herself a police car. Six others do the same (Leroy is the last: wanders in from his 'fishing trip', hands dripping in blood; telegrams the station). The police wonder how much more there might be. But the bloodshed stops on the seventh. Seven arrests for seven murders less than a few hours old, which at this point the press and (hence) public are still ignorant of.

In the next few days a picture is put together, by which time two Thanet nursing home suspects are dead, and dead from the c word. By christmas it transpires all seven had been quietly and terminally ill, and by christmas, all seven are dead.

Seven. A strange number, seven. Seven embittered and suffering old people without family and an indifference to organised religion venture out in their final days of frailing health with sadistic bloodlust and vain hope of procuring some twisted legacy? Maybe. But like the gardener discovering the weed in his vegetable patch is linked to a much larger web of activity, so our story has more to it than first meets the eye.

For the seven victims were not the usual targets of such sadistic murder (children, prostitutes, the elderly and so on - you will notice how such targets lack power). No, the seven discovered on the morning of the 1st, each killed by a respective patient of the Thanet nursing home, a crime which in their last few days of life, none of whom would provide any explanation of motive for, or for that matter, any input beyond a request for an extra blanket, a remark about the towering height of the investigating officer, refills of coffee, etc., - were not boys or girls or street workers, or women walking back from the town, but were in fact the seven richest men in the country of Great Britain at the time of the 1st of November 2031.

The deaths of the country's wealth-gifters were mourned greatly in the aftermath of the attacks. Economic recovery was slow, although there was indeed recovery, and by the beginning of the year 2032 the country was actually found to be better off than before (not because of the attacks, of course, but rather, a result of the random fluctuations economies are partial to, much like the weather).

It was said by some anti-business people that this demonstrated the superfluity of the plutocratic classes, given the murdered men were apparently removable with augmented consequences. One anti-business commentator even accused the men of performing a strange kind of robbery the people were used to. They claimed the men had lived in the country simply to avoid paying taxes found elsewhere, and were not really businessmen at all, but merely owners of many things and people.

Statues were promptly erected in retaliation, and such voices withered away accordingly.

*

On the 13th of April 2032, the Thanet Chess Club website was hijacked by Cyber-Terrorists. The home screen usually greeting visitors was turned into something far more sinister. The mauve background and tessellated rook piece motif was replaced with a neon insignia of a clenched fist, and the words 'NO PASARAN!'. The photograph of Pat Cummings lifting the seasonal winner's trophy was removed, and in its place were photographs of bodies. The seven, captured in grainy mobile phone footage. A new block of text, replacing the section, 'Updates on Last Week's Meeting', read:

On the 1st of November 2031 we murdered the seven richest people in the country of Great Britain.
On the 1st of November 2032 we will murder the seven richest people in the continent of Europe.
It is unfortunate for you we now have so little to lose.

The Thanet Chess Club committee was promptly arrested, though later released without charge. After an inconclusive investigation, the prevailing police theory was that the hijacking of the Thanet Chess Club website was a hoax. Still, an agreement was made with the media not to report on it, lest the wrong sorts be encouraged, or it should scare the good-god-fearing public. The website was shut down and apart from in a few circles of conspirators and masturbators, the hijacking gained no traction. It was brushed off as a tactless joke. That was of course until the morning of the 1st of November 2032.

*

The seven richest men in Europe had been warned of the Thanet Chess Club website hijacking but were urged to disregard it as the work of some sickly teenage boy with an excess of free time. Still, it cost nothing to be cautious (for the rich it never did), and so security was ramped up for the 1st of November 2032. The seven murdered the year before had been unsuspecting sitting ducks. This year it would take more than seven elderly c****r patients to take down seven men protected by armed security guards and dogs, tripwires and booby traps, as indeed the richest seven now were.

On the 1st of November 2032, Europe woke to a slaughter. The seven richest men in the continent had been murdered. In their beds, in their bunkers: their dogs and guards given the slip by temazepam-laced meats and pornos suspended on fishing lines.

Seven were promptly arrested due to the brave and strategic intervention of European intelligence services, but all swallowed cyanide capsules immediately after carrying out their executions and were dead by the time the cold steel of the handcuffs had coiled their wrists.

There was much speculation in the aftermath as to who these seven attackers were, and to which terrorist organisation they belonged (for the attacks were now terroristic, the media had ordained). A receipt paper for the Thanet Morrisons was discovered in the coat pocket of one of the attackers. He had been found hiding in the bushes of a golf course a well-reputed billionaire steel magnate was playing on. The terrorist had replaced the magnate's golf ball with one that exploded when hit with sufficient force. The magnate had struck the ball hard enough to spray himself all over the fourth hole, soddening his entourages clothing with red.

So Thanet was incriminated once again. Tourism suffered as the police made countless raids throughout the town in pursuit of the seven terrorists who they now had reason to believe hailed from the same place as their murderous predecessors. More than forty people were arrested, but nothing was found to link the suspects to the attacks, and all were later released with an apology from the investigators.

The media turned on the police. The earlier hijacking of the Thanet Chess Club website, and the morbid now accurate threat that had been distributed from it, was released to the public by one media mogul as evidence of police incompetence. There were calls for the resignations of senior officers who they claimed had been lackadaisical in pursuing the real and credible threats of a terroristic militia.

The Thanet Chess Club chairman, Jon Barnes, was forced into police protection. The public's deductions were that he must have been responsible for everything, as he had the website's password. The police calmed the demands for his execution by reassuring the public they had already investigated a certain Jon Barnes and found him to be in possession of an alibi for the last two November 1sts. On both occasions, he had been watching Eurovision song contests with his sister. Still, the scout hut in which the weekly chess meets were held, was torched, and meetings at the club were suspended for concerns of the safety of its members.

Switzerland - which lost two of its citizens in the European-wide attacks - called for trade restrictions on Britain until the terrorist threat had been taken care of. The Swiss ambassador suggested the attacks demonstrated Britain's underlying anti-business credentials; that the country could not be trusted in a highly competitive globalised market.

Everything changed on the 16th of April 2033.

The Thanet Chess Club website, which was now black-listed, went live again. "NO PASARAN!" and a clenched fist returned as backdrops. The text read:

On the 1st of November 2032 we fulfilled a promise to end the lives of the seven richest people in Europe.

Today we make the promise to end the lives of the world's seven richest people on the 1st of November 2033.

Remember we are quite capable of foregoing our flesh: you are not.

The Thanet Chess Club website was removed in minutes, by which time its ominous message had been shared tens of thousands of times over social media. The next day a screenshot of the threat appeared in every major newspaper around the world. "We will fight them on the beaches..." began the headline of the UK Daily Telegraph, which promised to smash terrorism wherever and whenever it reared its ugly head.

Then nothing happened for a couple of months.

The governments of the world formed a coalition, collectively agreeing to tackle the terrorist threat. In the meantime, life would go on as before. The public was warned that if it didn't, the terrorists would win. But behind the scenes militaristic and intelligence services were ramped up to unprecedented levels to get to the bottom of everything that might happen. Although progress with the investigation was slow, there was level-headedness among the population all the while. Many were convinced the last two November 1sts could not repeat themselves. This time, security really would be heightened, they thought. The world's richest would be encased in bomb-proof shelters, protected by whole armies, if they really needed to be, for that day.

The terrorists would not win.

But then something happened which was the catalyst for everything that happened after that. On the 27th of August 2033, Orimer Souleyman, who at that time was ranked the richest man in the world, decided he did not want to be a billionaire anymore. On that day he decided to relinquish a large portion of his wealth so that he might still be rich, but not so rich he would be the prime target for terrorists.

However, it is harder than you might think to get rid of billions. It is, first of all, a lot of money to spend; there are only so many pairs of shoes that can be worn on two feet, for instance. The money would have to be given away. But it was not easy to give away money in those days. Orimer's billionaire friends did not want the money in case they might inherit his position in the firing line. They were comfortable enough as they were, and Orimer's money would make them uncomfortable, they thought.

So Orimer did something clever with his unnecessary fortune. On the 27th of August 2033, he provided the gulf's migrant workforce with free education and healthcare. Then he entirely funded a high-speed railway connecting two of the biggest cities. He managed to rid himself, overnight, of a few billion dollars, improved the lives of millions, and could now sleep soundly knowing he was only the world's 60th richest or so, and no longer a target for a bitter militia that detested his successes.

Well, it was alright for Orimer, but now there was a new person in the world's richest seven; a person who probably did not want the honour. The second richest man had become the richest, and now they were all starting to feel a bit vulnerable, especially having seen their colleague Orimer's reaction to such a status.

Two days after Orimer Souleyman resigned his position at the top, the world's fourth-richest person, Oscar Blabakov (a Russian entrepreneur and oligarch) announced he would provide Zambia with a total rehaul of its road system. He paid off all of Angola's external debt. Blabakov shed a healthy $45 billion on these projects, which put him down to around the 200th spot on the rich list. In a press release, Blabakov insisted that his actions were in no way linked to the Thanet Chess Club threats, and were, instead, projects he had been interested in for a while.

Three weeks later and not one of the world's seven richest persons were the same as before. India now had a free public transport system. A pipeline was in the process of being built across sub-Saharan Africa, to provide every citizen with free VOSS water. The slums of Rio were dotted with cranes and mechanical diggers. The richest man in the world was a tenth as rich as he who had held that position a month earlier.

On the 3rd of October 2033, Orimer Souleyman was in the bath when he received a phone call from his accountant telling him he was the world's richest person once again. "Yikes!" he cried, sputtering champagne over his huge marble floor. "But I gave so much of it away!" Later that day Orimer got rid of the lot: everything except a modest five-bedroom house, two range rovers and $100,000 in cash: enough to live the life of a nobody, he thought, but pretty well.

Well, the panic was now fully in motion. As October neared to an end, much of the world looked like a building site, as homes and infrastructure seemed to grow out of the ground for the world's poorest. It was all quite fantastic. In America and Europe, the media continued to talk about coalitions and terrorists, but the words were starting to lose sway with the public. Life seemed to be getting better in spite of the doom forecast by the papers, and the stocks that dropped massively each day. Common people moved into large apartments on the river banks of capital cities, which had previously been empty. Not one person in Britain was homeless. The NHS now offered free plastic surgery, and scout groups went on field trips to the Grand Canyon and tropical rainforests of South America. Global warming had been set in reverse through innovative investments. There were free balloon rides. Work continued as 'a thing', but it was superfluous, existing mainly to fulfil a need to do something between the hours of 9 and 17, and to excuse all the street partying that now took place in the evenings.

One Swiss businessman, desperate to rid himself of the wealth he had stored up in gold coins, dumped them into a lake by his mansion. They worked their way down the waterfalls and out into the sea, and now the sea had a golden shimmer. Everything was becoming so beautiful.

The 1st of November 2033 came around, and the world braced itself for whatever the day might bring with it. The richest person that day was a man called Kashif Osmani, who owned an orphanage in Lahore. Kashif had no security guards (no one had enough wealth in those days for the sub-servitude of another human being), or dogs. He did not even carry a penknife with which he could protect himself. Instead, he kissed his wife and three children goodbye and went up a hill outside of the city to wait.

The world waited.

And on the 2nd of November 2033 Kashif Osmani returned from his hill, tired and hungry, looking forward to breakfast. No one had died, at least not in the devilish way our story concerns. There was much speculation as to why not: the people checked the Thanet Chess Club website for answers, but found it was offline.

*

A year later, after some changes were made regarding those who held power, it emerged that Jon Barnes, chairman of the Thanet Chess Club, had been the figurehead of the terroristic militia spawned in his hometown of Thanet that had murdered fourteen people. Barnes was an expert in evading police questioning, having given investigators the slip using his powers of lying well. No arrests were made, however, and no charges pressed, and to the contrary some even suggested that a statue be built in his honour, to commemorate what some were calling the: THANET CHESS CLUB REVOLUTION. The statue idea was rejected, however, as it was decided that sort of behaviour should not be encouraged again.

The militant wing of the Thanet Chess Club subsequently disbanded, and the organisation returned primarily to weekly chess. But the habits of the past never made a return, and anyone who felt they had been even slightly too greedy one year awaited the 1st of November with superstitious nervousness and a propensity for charity.

Our story ends there, as I say, the happiest in our history. It did not involve the kiss of a prince, or the death of some pointless spinster to procure the happy ending. Do not listen too well to the stories of your elders. Murder was the tool of our liberation: when the rich shared our fears the world become a place where we could all live happily ever after, forever and ever, Amen.

Sam Mills

Writer and haikuist
samuel.rutishausermills@gmail.com

Corey Mcallen

Illustrator and graphic designer
Email: mc-corey@hotmail.com
Insta: coreymcallen
cargocollective.com/mcallenillustration

Printed in Great Britain
by Amazon